Written but Never Sent

poems for the words we almost said

Liliana Caliente-Cazadora

Written but Never Sent

poems for the words we almost said

X

@CazadoraLiliana

author-liliana.com

Dedication

For the ones I never said it to.
And the ones who never said it back.
You still live in these pages.

For anyone who whispered the truth into a pillow,
typed out the message and deleted it,
or carried a goodbye that never got said—
this is for you.

Table of Contents

.

Introduction

This book is a collection of echoes.

It's made of late-night thoughts left unsent, words swallowed in silence, and truths that were never brave enough to leave my lips. Some of these poems were letters I wrote and deleted. Others were only imagined, rehearsed in my head a thousand times but never spoken aloud. Each one is a moment I lived quietly—too fragile to share at the time, but too honest to bury forever.

Written but Never Sent is for the people I couldn't confront, the love I couldn't hold onto, the pain I tried to package as poetry. It's for everyone who has ever stared at a blinking cursor, hovered over "send," and backed away. It's for those who've carried conversations in their chest for years. For those who still rehearse apologies. For those who were brave enough to feel it all but not reckless enough to say it.

You won't find perfect closure here. But you might find yourself.

So read slowly. Read late. Read when the world is quiet enough to hear what's been waiting inside you.

And if you've ever left something unsaid,
you are not alone.

—Liliana

SECTION I:
The Things We Never Said
Whispers, regrets, and the ache of unsent truths

To the One I Loved in Silence
by Liliana Caliente-Cazadora

I saw you when the world was gray and bare,
A flicker in the fog, a light so true.
You passed me by with sunlight in your hair,
Unknowing all the storms you pulled me through.

I wrote your name on corners of my mind,
In margins where my dreams would come and go.
You never looked, but still I hoped to find
A glance from you beneath the evening's glow.

You laughed, and I grew smaller in my skin,
A whisper lost beneath your gentle roar.
I traced the shape of love I held within—
A secret sealed behind a locked heart's door.

You spoke to me as though I were the breeze,
A soft companion drifting through your day.
But I, a stone sunk deep in silent seas,
Could never find the strength to make you stay.

So now I send this letter to the sky,
To vanish in the hush of falling snow.
I loved you once—but silence passed me by,
And now you'll never, ever have to know.

To My Childhood Bully
by Liliana Caliente-Cazadora

You laughed while pulling at my hair,
And called me names with practiced glee.
You chased me down the classroom stair,
A shadow I could never flee.

You mocked my clothes, my voice, my face,
And drew your joy from every tear.
Your words still echo, leave a trace—
A whisper I refused to hear.

But time, dear foe, has changed the scene.
I found the power you denied.
Your hate once made me small, unseen—
Now all your chains have come untied.

I learned to speak with steady grace,
To stand though fear still shakes my spine.
You left a bruise I can't erase,
But not a soul that you define.

So here's the truth I never said:
You hurt me, yes—but I survived.
And though you lived inside my head,
It's me, not you, who has arrived.

To the Stranger Who Saved Me
by Liliana Caliente-Cazadora

You didn't know the storm behind my eyes,
The way my world was cracking at the seams.
I wore a smile, but underneath were lies—
A drowning heart that no one heard or sees.

We met for seconds on a crowded street.
You caught my gaze and smiled without a word.
So small a thing, and yet the act was sweet—
A moment seen, a soul at last occurred.

You held the door. You said my name just right.
You didn't flinch when tears welled up in mine.
You saw me there, alone and locked in fight,
And offered warmth without a grand design.

You'll never know the part you chose to play.
You'll never see the thread you gently tied.
But something in me shifted on that day—
The part that wanted, once again, to try.

So thank you, stranger—silent, kind, and true.
You gave me back a breath I thought was gone.
And though I never got to speak to you,
Your simple grace still pulls me gently on.

To the Girl I Used to Be
by Liliana Caliente-Cazadora

You tried to smile while biting back the pain,
And danced for love you never thought you'd earn.
You faced the world through heartbreak and through rain,
But no one taught you how to crash and turn.

You traced your worth in others' fickle hands,
And begged for scraps beneath their pointed gaze.
You didn't know that love commands no brands,
And still you hoped through all your silent days.

I see you now, so fragile yet so fierce,
A spark still burning in your shadowed eyes.
You stood though doubt would claw and shame would pierce—
A warrior cloaked in sweet, uncertain lies.

I wish I'd held you closer in those years,
And whispered truths you needed to believe:
That joy is not the absence of your tears,
And strength is found in learning how to grieve.

You were enough, though no one told you so.
You mattered, though the world refused to see.
And now I write the words you'll never know—
With love, from who you helped me grow to be.

To the Year That Broke Me
by Liliana Caliente-Cazadora

You dragged me through the fire, day by day,
And carved your name in every breath I took.
You tore my steady ground and walked away,
Leaving a soul unraveling by the book.

You dressed in death and silence, grief and stone,
Each sunrise colder than the one before.
You made the world feel distant, vast, unknown—
A maze with shattered glass across the floor.

You taught me fear in ways I'd never known,
And burned my joy like paper in the rain.
You showed me how it feels to be alone,
To sit with ghosts and memorize their names.

And yet, somehow, I made it to the end—
Not whole, not healed, but breathing all the same.
Each scar you left has now become a friend,
A mark that tells the truth beneath the shame.

You didn't win, though God, you tried to take
The last of me, the softest part I had.
But I have learned what strength it takes to break—
And rise again from ashes, bruised, but glad.

To the Dream I Gave Up
by Liliana Caliente-Cazadora

I held you like a flame against the night,
A secret wish I whispered into air.
You shimmered just beyond my grasping sight,
A promise spun from hope and quiet prayer.

I shaped my world around the thought of you,
And colored all my days with what could be.
You gave my restless heart a path to view,
A sky to chase, a softer place to flee.

But life is not so kind to fragile things,
And time grew heavy in my trembling hands.
The road was paved with shattered, stolen wings—
A trail of "almosts" lost in shifting sands.

I had to let you go to breathe again,
To make more room for love, for change, for rest.
It broke me more than words can hold or pen,
But sometimes giving up is for the best.

Still, now and then, I see you in the dark—
A flicker near the edge of sleep or rain.
You were my once, my guiding, golden spark…
The dream I lost, yet never loved in vain.

To My Anxiety

by Liliana Caliente-Cazadora

You wake me with a whisper sharp and low,
A voice that's mine, yet not the one I trust.
You follow me wherever I may go,
And turn my calmest moments into dust.

You taught my breath to tremble in my chest,
My hands to shake beneath the weightless air.
You dress in what I fear and what I've guessed,
Then laugh when all I feel is cold despair.

You steal the peace from rooms I once called mine,
And paint the walls with questions, doubt, and dread.
You twist my thoughts into a tangled line,
And feast on every tear I've ever shed.

But I have learned your tricks, your steady lies.
I've named you now and seen the way you feed.
You shrink beneath the light that truth applies—
You vanish when I no longer concede.

So here's your note: I'm done with playing host.
You're not my friend, though once you wore the name.
I'm learning how to walk without your ghost,
And I won't bow each time you call in shame.

To the Words I Couldn't Say Out Loud
by Liliana Caliente-Cazadora

You sat behind my teeth
like prisoners—
pacing, pacing, pacing.

You were heavy with meaning,
bloated with urgency,
but I swallowed you
because silence
was safer
than judgment.

I felt you climb my throat at midnight
when the lights were off
and the past came knocking,
asking why I let it happen,
why I didn't scream,
why I nodded when I should've run.

You curled into the corners of my journals,
bleeding ink instead of breath.
You showed up in poems
masquerading as metaphors,
softening your shape
so no one would know
you were real.

You were the apology
I rehearsed for years
and never gave.
The truth
I owed myself
but didn't think I deserved.

The "I love you"
I let die
in the space between glances.

I want you to know—
I see you now.
I name you without flinching.
You were never weak.
You were never too much.
You were mine.

And though I never spoke you
in the moment,
you lived.
You mattered.
And you are free now.

To the Apology I'll Never Receive

by Liliana Caliente-Cazadora

You should have come
with eyes lowered,
hands open—
not to erase what happened,
but to acknowledge it.

You should have said,
"I was wrong."
"I hurt you."
"I see it now."

But you never did.

Instead, you vanished into
other people's versions of you,
cleaned up your name
and scrubbed me from the story.
You moved on—
like I was just
a bad day you forgot to feel.

But I carried it.
I carried the silence,
the gaslight,
the ache of wanting truth
from someone who only ever
spoke to win.

You don't know
how many nights I stood
in front of a mirror,
rehearsing your lines for you—

whispering your sorrys
so I could sleep.

You'll never speak them.
I've stopped waiting.
And somehow,
I've started healing anyway.

Because I no longer need
your mouth to form
what I already knew.

I was worthy of the apology.
Even if you were never
brave enough
to give it.

To the One Who Ghosted Me
by Liliana Caliente-Cazadora

You left like a window
slamming shut in a storm—
quick,
loud,
final.

No warning.
No goodbye.
Just silence
where your name used to echo.

I kept checking my phone
like it might apologize for you,
like it might fill in the blanks
your absence carved into me.

What did I say wrong?
Was I too much,
or not enough?
Did I make you feel seen—
and that scared you?
Or did I not matter at all?

I replayed our last conversation
so many times
it started to sound like static.

You didn't owe me forever,
but you owed me something.
A sentence.
A reason.
A truth.

Instead,
I became a ghost too—
haunting old messages,
wondering if I'd imagined us.

But here's what you didn't take:
my voice.
My worth.
The part of me that still believes
some people mean what they say
and stay when it's hard.

You disappeared—
but I didn't.
I'm still here.
And I won't vanish
just because you did.

To the Love That Almost Was
by Liliana Caliente-Cazadora

We never called it love.
Not out loud.
Not with words.

But we felt it—
in the way your hand hovered near mine
for a second too long,
in the way we laughed
like we'd known each other
in other lives.

There was something there,
wasn't there?
That glimmer of maybe,
of what if,
of not yet.

You were the breath
before the kiss that never came.
The echo of a song
that never played
but still got stuck in my head.

I remember you
in moments,
not milestones—
a coffee shared,
a joke that only we understood,
your eyes when they softened,
almost brave enough
to say what we both knew.

But we chose the safe path.
The polite silence.
The long goodbye
that pretended to be nothing at all.

And still—
sometimes—
I wonder who we could have been
if one of us
had just
spoken first.

To My Ex on the Day You Married Someone Else
by Liliana Caliente-Cazadora

I saw the photo.
You looked happy.
Your smile was real—
not the one you wore
when we were unraveling
but too afraid to admit it.

She held your hand
the way I used to,
but lighter,
as if love never had to be
heavy or hard.

And I thought I'd be wrecked.
I thought the weight of your tux
and her white dress
would crush the last
of what I still held onto.

But instead,
I just sat there,
holding a cup of coffee
and memories
that no longer burned.

We were never meant
to make it past the fire.
We mistook sparks for warmth,
flames for forever.
And maybe we needed to—
to learn what love isn't
before we could find what it is.

So I didn't cry.
Not this time.
I just whispered a blessing
to the version of you
that once held my heart—
and to the version of me
that let it go.

May she love you
in the ways I couldn't.
May you love her
without all the ghosts
we left behind.

And may I keep walking forward,
not bitter,
not broken,
just free.

SECTION II:
Written but Never Sent
Messages drafted, deleted, or delivered in silence

Unsent Email at 2:14 AM
by Liliana Caliente-Cazadora

Subject: (no subject)
To: (still you)

I don't even know why I'm writing this.
You won't read it.
Hell, I won't send it.
But here I am—2:14 a.m.,
staring at this blinking cursor
like it owes me closure.

I thought I was over you.
I say that a lot.
Loudly, sometimes.
Like the louder I say it,
the truer it might become.

But tonight,
I saw someone who walked like you.
Not exactly—but enough
to punch the air out of me.
Enough to remember
how your laugh used to fill the quiet
and how your absence
echoes louder than your voice ever did.

There are things I never told you.
Not because I couldn't—
but because I knew you'd leave
if I did.
So I swallowed those truths
like pills I didn't believe in.
I smiled. I nodded.

I made it easy to walk away.
You're welcome.

I don't want you back.
I just want
you to feel
for one second
what it was like
to love someone
who treated your heart
like a maybe.

Anyway.
Delete this.
Or don't.
It's not really for you, is it?
It never was.

—Liliana

Voicemail I Never Left

by Liliana Caliente-Cazadora

—beep—

Hey.
It's... me.
You probably knew that—
I guess the number still shows up.
Unless you've deleted me.

Um...
I don't really know
why I'm calling.

I mean,
I do.
I just—

I was thinking about that night
we sat in your car
with the windows down,
not saying much,
but it felt like everything.
Remember that?
God, maybe you don't.

I thought I was okay.
I've been okay.
Mostly.

But tonight
I heard that song—
our song, I guess,
if we were ever allowed to have one.

And I felt it all over again,
like the memory had teeth.

I'm not asking for anything.
Not to come back.
Not to fix it.
Not even to talk.

I just wanted you to know
you mattered.

You still do.

And I never said goodbye.

...

Anyway.
Forget it.
I'm not even going to—

—*message deleted*—

Postcards from My Heart
by Liliana Caliente-Cazadora

Paris, Early Spring
I saw a woman who wore your scent.
I followed her for two blocks—
not because I thought it was you,
but because I missed what it felt like
to breathe without aching.

Seattle, Rainy Tuesday
You would've loved this café.
Dim lights. Old jazz. Mismatched mugs.
I ordered your drink.
It still tastes like almost.

New York, Alone in a Crowd
I passed a couple holding hands—
she bumped into him, and he smiled
like nothing else existed.
I almost smiled too.
Then remembered
we never quite fit like that.

Arizona, My Childhood Bedroom
I found our letters
in a shoebox beneath my old bed.
Your handwriting looks like hope
and apology
and a promise I'm glad you didn't keep.

Chicago, Two Drinks In
If I called you now,
would your voice still curl around my name
like it used to?

Don't worry—
I won't.
But God, I thought about it.

Home, Tonight
I am learning
to send love
without a return address.
And most days,
that feels like enough.

Group Chat Left on Read
by Liliana Caliente-Cazadora

[9:03 PM] me:
hey y'all
you good? just checking in

[9:06 PM] seen by: Jess, Riley, Ana, Cam
(no reply)

[9:12 PM] me:
lol
ignore me I guess
just one of *those* nights lol

[9:18 PM] me:
actually
nvm
I'm fine

[9:27 PM] seen by: Jess
(no reply)

[9:41 PM] me (unsent message):
I miss who we were
before the world turned loud and everyone
learned to pretend they're okay in 12 emojis or less

[9:55 PM] me:
anyone want to hang out this weekend?

[10:17 PM] seen by: Riley, Cam, Ana
(no reply)

My phone glows
like it's trying to warm me,
but it only burns.

There's something cruel
about being left on read—
it's not silence,
it's acknowledgement
without engagement.
Like someone looked
right through you
and still decided
you weren't worth
a thumbtap back.

[10:45 PM] me:
never mind lol
I'm gonna head to bed
love you guys 🖤

[10:46 PM] seen by: Everyone
(no reply)

Some ghosts don't haunt you.
They just scroll past
and forget you were ever alive
in the first place.

Drafts Folder
by Liliana Caliente-Cazadora

Subject: Just checking in
Saved: 1:02 AM
Hey...
I don't know why I'm writing.
I guess I just
miss the way we used to talk
about nothing and everything
until it all blurred.
Are you sleeping okay?
I'm not.
(never sent)

Subject: Sorry
Saved: 3:14 PM
I was angry.
Not just at you.
At the world.
At myself.
At how easy it was for you to move on
while I stayed behind,
trying to forgive both of us.
I didn't mean half of what I said.
But the other half still hurts.
(never sent)

Subject: Do you remember...
Saved: 11:47 PM
...that night in the kitchen?
When the power went out
and we lit candles
and talked like
the world wasn't falling apart?
I go back to that moment more than I should.
It's the one that convinces me
we were real.
(never sent)

Subject: Closure
Saved: 9:21 AM
Actually—
forget it.
If I have to ask for closure,
it's not real closure, is it?
Just another wound
I've learned to live around.
(never sent)

Subject: (blank)
Saved: 2:39 AM
You
You
You
You
You
You
(never sent)

Subject: None of this matters
Saved: Draft deleted
(No recovery available)

Fill in the Blanks
by Liliana Caliente-Cazadora

I still remember _____,
and the way you _____
when no one else was watching.

You said _____,
but I heard something else entirely.

The last thing I wanted to say was _____,
but instead I said _____
because I thought it would hurt less.

I never told you about _____.
I kept it hidden, folded beneath _____.

You left on a _____ kind of day,
and the air smelled like _____.
That detail still haunts me.

Sometimes, when I can't sleep,
I picture _____.
It makes it worse. Or better.
I still can't decide.

If I could speak to you now,
I'd say:
"_____."

But you're not listening.
And maybe you never were.

Return to Sender
by Liliana Caliente-Cazadora

I loved you more than I admitted to myself.
Even now, I flinch at your name.
Return to sender—recipient unknown.

I'm sorry I never said goodbye.
But you didn't either.
Return to sender—recipient unknown.

I stayed silent when I should've screamed.
It didn't make me strong. Just quiet.
Return to sender—recipient unknown.

I blamed you for leaving,
but part of me had already let go first.
Return to sender—recipient unknown.

You said I was hard to love.
I carried that like gospel.
Return to sender—recipient unknown.

I still have the gift I never gave you.
Wrapped in dust and maybe.
Return to sender—recipient unknown.

Sometimes I draft a message just to delete it.
Just to feel like I'm saying something.
Return to sender—recipient unknown.

I forgive you.
Not for you—
for me.
Return to sender—recipient unknown.

SECTION III:
Experimental Echoes
Emotions reframed through modern forms and metaphors

Choose Your Own Emotion
by Liliana Caliente-Cazadora

You see them at the grocery store.
They look the same, but you don't.
You freeze.
Your heart does that stupid flutter thing.
You have three options:

---

1. If you say "hello," turn to stanza two.
2. If you walk away, skip to stanza five.
3. If you smile like a stranger and mean it, go to stanza eight.

[Stanza Two – You Say Hello]

Your voice cracks on their name.
They smile like nothing ever happened.
You talk about weather.
You talk about time.
You don't talk about
the thing that wrecked you.

They ask how you've been.
You have two choices:

→ If you tell them the truth, turn to stanza three.
→ If you lie and say "I'm good," skip to stanza four.

[Stanza Three – You Tell the Truth]

You say: "I wasn't okay for a long time."
It hangs in the air like fog,
but they don't flinch.
They nod.
Say they weren't either.

For a second,
it's almost like healing.
Not reunion. Not closure.
But something like mutual forgiveness.

You both smile—
not the fake kind.
Then walk away
lighter.

[Stanza Four – You Say 'I'm Good']

They smile.
You smile.
Two liars in the snack aisle.

You part ways,
and it feels like a breakup
you already had
but still managed to relive.

You wonder
why you still care
when they clearly don't.

[Stanza Five – You Walk Away]

You turn down Aisle 5.
Pick up cereal you don't need.
Pretend your hands aren't shaking.
Later, you'll say
you were the strong one.
You'll almost believe it.

A voice calls your name from behind.
It's them.
You have two options:

→ **If you keep walking, skip to stanza six.**
→ **If you stop and turn around, go to stanza seven.**

[Stanza Six – You Keep Walking]

You never look back.
Not then. Not after.
You carry the ache with pride—
a scar you choose to keep.

You'll replay it later,
but at least the story stayed yours.
Unfinished,
but yours.

[Stanza Seven – You Turn Around]

They ask, "Was that you?"
You say it was.
They say they didn't expect to see you.

It feels polite.
Forced.
Like two actors
who've forgotten the script
but still have to finish the scene.

You smile. They smile.
And just like that,
you remember
why it ended.

[Stanza Eight – You Smile Like a Stranger]

It's the cleanest pain.
The softest kind of goodbye.
They nod. You nod.
Like two people
who used to know each other
in another life
where things almost worked.

You could stop there.
But your hand lingers
on your phone in the parking lot.

You have two options:

→ **If you send a text afterward, go to stanza nine.**
→ **If you drive away in silence, skip to stanza ten.**

[Stanza Nine – You Text Them Later]

"Good to see you."
You stare at the message.
Hit send.
Immediately regret it.

Three dots appear.
Then disappear.

You turn off your phone
before it can
hurt you again.

[Stanza Ten – You Drive Away in Silence]

Music plays on the radio,
but you don't hear it.

For once,
you let a moment pass
without trying to make it mean more.

You were brave
in your stillness.
And somehow,
that's enough.

End of Game.
But not the end of you.

You'll see them again—
in your dreams,
in a song,
in the silence between other people's words.

And next time,
you'll choose differently.
Or maybe you won't.

Either way,
you'll survive it.

Recalculating: A Route to Closure
by Liliana Caliente-Cazadora

Starting route to: Closure
Head north through Denial.
In 0.3 miles, turn left onto What If.
Continue straight through Memory Lane—
expect unexpected stops.

In 500 feet,
pass by the place you last saw them.
Avoid eye contact with the version of yourself
that still thinks they'll come back.

Caution: Road may be slippery with tears.
Take a sharp right at Acceptance
(it will not look like you imagined).

At the roundabout,
ignore the urge to loop through Old Messages.
Stay right to merge onto
"I Did My Best" Blvd.

In 2 miles,
continue through the Tunnels of Silence.
You will feel lost. That's part of it.
Keep going.

Construction ahead:
Heart under repair.
Delays are expected. Be patient.

In 1,000 feet,
you'll reach the intersection of Letting Go and Moving Forward.
Turn slowly. Use both hands.

Your destination will be on the right.
It will not be lit.
It may not feel like home.

But it is yours.

You have arrived.

If you need a new destination,
I'm still here.
Ready to recalculate.

FRAGILE: HANDLE WITH CARE
by Liliana Caliente-Cazadora

Shipping Label: One (1) Heart
Status: Previously Loved
Condition: Pre-fractured
Contents may shift during transit.

Item Description:
• 100% human sorrow
• Edges worn from overuse
• Still beating, somehow

Handling Instructions:
☐ Do not bend the truth
☐ Do not crush beneath indifference
☐ Do not expose to sudden silence or unspoken goodbyes

This item may include:
– Unread letters
– Ghosted messages
– A playlist that still hurts
– One last apology (unopened)

Warning:
Product may leak at night.

Do not shake.
Memories inside are not secured.

Return Policy:
No refunds.
No exchanges.
Keep it only if you mean to keep it well.

Stamp:
FRAGILE
this heart has already survived
more than it should have.
please
don't
be
the reason
it doesn't
again.

THE CONVERSATION THAT NEVER HAPPENED
by Liliana Caliente-Cazadora

INT. KITCHEN – NIGHT
Low light. A single lamp hums.
Two mugs sit on the counter, untouched.
SHE stands at the sink, hands braced on porcelain.
HE leans in the doorway, arms crossed.
They do not look at each other.

SHE:
So, are you going to say something?

HE:
What do you want me to say?

SHE:
Anything real.
Anything that sounds like you meant to stay.

(beat)

HE:
I didn't know how to stay
without losing myself.

SHE:
And I didn't know how to let go
without losing everything else.

(long pause)

HE:
You were never the problem.

SHE:
But I became the consequence.

(beat)

HE:
Sometimes I still hear your voice
when I'm not even trying to.

SHE:
I stopped speaking in ways
that could echo.

(she looks at him)
I wanted you to fight for me.
Even just once.

HE:
I didn't think I could win.

SHE:
You didn't even try.

(silence grows loud)

HE:
I wish I could change it.

SHE:
So do I.
But wishes aren't actions,
and silence isn't love.

(she walks past him)

HE:
Wait—
Would it have mattered
if I said I still loved you?

SHE (softly):
Not anymore.

FADE TO BLACK

This Is Where I Leave You
by Liliana Caliente-Cazadora

This is where I leave you—
at the edge of a sentence
I was never brave enough to finish.

You were always more silence
than sound,
more maybe
than yes.

I begged the universe for signs,
and it answered in whispers
I pretended to understand.

We mistook timing
for destiny.
Mistook comfort
for love.

And I—
I mistook you
for forever.

I held on too long.
Not to you,
but to the version of me
that loved you
at all costs.

I see now
you were only a chapter.
But I kept rereading it

like it held the ending
I needed.

It didn't.

You are not my future.
You are not my unfinished poem.
You are just
the part I finally let go of.

This is where I leave you.

Baggage Claim
by Liliana Caliente-Cazadora

Welcome to the terminal
of things I've carried too long.

Please stand clear of the carousel.
Some of this might still explode.

Bag #01 – Guilt
Overpacked.
Contents: every word I didn't say,
every word I said wrong.
Tag reads: "Should've known better."

Bag #07 – Abandonment Issues
Unclaimed since childhood.
Still circles the belt,
asking everyone if they'll stay.

Bag #12 – Your Hoodie
Still smells like forgiveness.
Still fits.
But I can't wear it anymore.

Bag #19 – Apologies (Unsent)
Lightweight, but heavy where it matters.

Zipper stuck.
Labeled: "Drafts Folder."

Bag #23 – That One Night
Looks fine on the outside.
Inside:
a cracked phone,
a broken promise,
a voicemail never deleted.

Bag #30 – Self-Worth
Left behind by accident.
Surprised to see it again.
It looks different now.
A little worn, but finally mine.

Bag #35 – You
Checked you at the gate.
Didn't realize how much space you took
until I started walking
without you.

All baggage claimed.
Nothing left spinning.
Nothing left behind
that I still need to carry.

Flight to Somewhere New
is boarding now.

Missed Call History
by Liliana Caliente-Cazadora

▦ Call Log – You

2:14 AM – Missed call
I almost said your name out loud in the dark.
Did you hear it anyway?

2:17 AM – No voicemail
Silence has never sounded so much like you.

2:31 AM – Missed call
I wanted to tell you I'm sorry.
Instead, I hung up on the ringing.

3:05 AM – Missed call
I remembered the way you laughed
when you were tired and honest.
I tried not to.

3:28 AM – Missed call
I just wanted to hear your voice.
Even your recorded one.
Even the one that says, "Leave a message."

3:52 AM – Missed call
This one wasn't about you.
It was about me.
Needing something. Anything.

4:00 AM – Voicemail recorded (not sent)
"I loved you. I still do. I'm trying not to."
Deleted.

4:01 AM – Missed call
I let the phone ring until it stopped feeling like you.

Battery low.
Signal weak.
Heart still calling.

PASSWORD RESET REQUEST
by Liliana Caliente-Cazadora

Username:
heart.in.recovery

Email associated with account:
leftbehind@almostlove.com

Security Questions:
• What did they call you when they meant it?
　　Answer: _____

• Where did they leave you?
　　Answer: between a sentence and a silence

• What was your last shared lie?
　　Answer: "I'm okay."

Verification Code Sent To:
a phone number you deleted
but still remember by heart

Enter New Password:
Must include at least:

- One moment of honesty

- One capital letter you never sent

- One symbol of what's been broken

- One number of nights you didn't sleep

　New Password: _____hopefulAgain_23?

Confirm New Password:

New Password: _____hopefulAgain_23?

ERROR:
Passwords don't match.
Try again.

TERMS & CONDITIONS
by Liliana Caliente-Cazadora

Love Agreement v.2.0
Last updated: the moment you smiled and meant it

BY OPENING THIS HEART, YOU AGREE TO THE FOLLOWING TERMS:

1. You will not ghost me after I've shown you the softest parts of myself.

2. You will not use my secrets against me, even in silence.

3. You acknowledge that this heart is not new.
   It has survived previous users, unexpected shutdowns, and emotional malware.

SECTION I: ACCEPTANCE OF TERMS
Your presence implies consent.
Your silence will be interpreted as rejection.
Mixed signals will be treated as loss of signal.

SECTION II: WARRANTY DISCLAIMER
This heart comes with no guarantees—
but it beats honest,
loves deep,
and tries hard not to give up,
even when it should.

SECTION III: LIMITATION OF LIABILITY

You are not responsible
for the damage you didn't mean to cause.
But you are still accountable.

SECTION IV: TERMINATION

This agreement may be terminated
without notice,
without closure,
without justice.

Side effects of termination may include:

- late-night overthinking

- memory loops

- dry throat when saying your name

- the unshakable need to text you and delete it before sending

SECTION V: GOVERNING EMOTIONS

This contract is governed by vulnerability,
hope,
and that one version of me
that still believed you'd stay.

By continuing, you accept all risks.
Including the risk
that I might love you
more than you're ready for.

[ ] I Agree
[ ] I Shouldn't

Emotional Autocorrect
by Liliana Caliente-Cazadora

Typed: I miss you.
Autocorrected: I'm good, thanks.

Typed: I still love you.
Autocorrected: Hope you're doing well.

Typed: I wish things were different.
Autocorrected: No regrets.

Typed: I'm hurting.
Autocorrected: Just tired.

Typed: I wanted forever.
Autocorrected: I knew it wouldn't last.

Typed: I forgive you.
Autocorrected: Whatever.

Typed: Please come back.
Autocorrected: Take care.

Typed: I meant what I said.
Autocorrected: It was nothing.

Typed: I need you.
Autocorrected: I'm fine.

Typed: I'm not fine.
Autocorrected: I'm fine.

Typed: I don't know who I am without you.
Autocorrected: I'm figuring it out.

Typed: I'm still broken.
Autocorrected: I'm healing.
Typed again: I'm healing.
Autocorrected: Maybe.

Typing...
by Liliana Caliente-Cazadora

[8:47 PM] me:
hey

[8:48 PM] me:
you around?

[8:52 PM] seen
(no reply)

[8:59 PM] me:
it's probably dumb
just
felt like saying hi

[9:01 PM] me (unsent):
I miss you more than I admit to myself

[9:03 PM] me:
do you ever
think about that night on the roof?

[9:05 PM] me:
nevermind
you're probably busy
or asleep
or just done

[9:10 PM] me:
I was going to tell you something
but I think I'll just write it in my head
like always

[9:12 PM] me (typing…)
(delete)
(typing…)
(delete again)

[9:18 PM] me:
anyway
hope you're good

[9:19 PM] me:
I mean that
even if you never say anything back

[9:20 PM] seen
(no reply)

[9:27 PM] me:
okay
guess that's all
goodnight

[9:28 PM] me:
still love you
(sorry)
(delete)

RECEIPT FOR WHAT LOVE COST ME
by Liliana Caliente-Cazadora

Liliana's Heartstop Mart
1234 Regret Lane
Somewhere, USA
Date: Unknown
Time: Too Late

ITEMS PURCHASED

Hope (unreciprocated).............. $4.99
Words I Shouldn't Have Swallowed.. $9.00
"I'm Fine" (Fake Smile Bundle)..... $3.33
Forgiveness (On Clearance)......... $2.22
Midnight Tears (Box of 12)......... $6.00
Ignored Texts (Read but Unseen).... $5.75
Overthinking (Economy Size)....... $11.11
Self-Worth (Traded In)............. $0.00
Dreams Deferred (2-for-1 Deal)..... $7.50
Memories I Can't Return............ Priceless

SUBTOTAL......................... $49.90
TAX (Emotional Damage).......... $12.76

TOTAL............................ $62.66
PAID............................ With My Peace

CHANGE GIVEN.................... None
BALANCE DUE...................... Still Hurting

Thank you for shopping with us.
Please come again. Or don't.

[REDACTED LETTER FOUND IN A DESK DRAWER]
by Liliana Caliente-Cazadora

Dear [REDACTED],

I never meant to
[REDACTED]
but the way you looked at me
that night
under the [REDACTED]
I think I knew.

You asked me
if I ever felt real love—
I said
[REDACTED]
but what I meant was
yes.

I still remember
your hands
[REDACTED]
the silence after
you left
like a shadow
stitched to my skin.

I should have said
I was sorry
for the things I didn't say.

I should have said
I loved you
[REDACTED]
but my mouth

was a locked room
and the key
was buried beneath
everything I was afraid to lose.

If this ever reaches you—
know that the part of me
that could never forget
still
hasn't.

With all the things
I couldn't write,
[L]

SECTION IV:
The Letting Go

Soft exits, whispered goodbyes, and quiet reclamation

To God, If You're Still Listening
by Liliana Caliente-Cazadora

To God, if you're still listening through the night,
I've whispered prayers with no reply to show.
My faith is flickering, but holds on tight.

The world feels dark, and nothing's going right—
I seek your face in places I don't go.
To God, if you're still listening through the night,

I used to think your love would feel like light,
But now it feels like silence wrapped in snow.
My faith is flickering, but holds on tight.

I've asked for peace instead of strength to fight,
And questioned why you let me fall so low.
To God, if you're still listening through the night,

Forgive the times I doubted wrong from right,
And begged for signs the sky refused to show.
My faith is flickering, but holds on tight.

If you are near, then guide my soul in flight,
And help me bloom where bitter winds still blow.
To God, if you're still listening through the night—
My faith is flickering, but holds on tight.

To the Universe That Forgot Me
by Liliana Caliente-Cazadora

I reached for stars that never reached for me,
A name unspoken in your endless sky.
You spun, unmoved, in cold eternity.

I whispered dreams into infinity,
But silence met me—no reply, no why.
I reached for stars that never reached for me.

The planets danced with careless dignity,
While I stood small, too quiet to defy
Your spinning, unmoved, cold eternity.

I prayed to something, anything, to see
The ache I carried, how I used to try.
I reached for stars that never reached for me.

Did you forget? Or were you always free
Of duty to the ones who cry and die—
You spun, unmoved, in cold eternity.

Yet still I write, though you will never be
The arms I hoped would catch me from the sky.
I reached for stars that never reached for me—
You spun, unmoved, in cold eternity.

To the Silence After You Left
by Liliana Caliente-Cazadora

The silence settled deeper than the pain,
A ghost that clung to every breath and wall.
You vanished, and the stillness made it plain.

No slammed door, no excuse to help explain—
Just absence, like a fog that would not fall.
The silence settled deeper than the pain.

I listened for your steps, but none remain.
I called, but only heard my own footfall.
You vanished, and the stillness made it plain.

The house became a shrine I couldn't feign—
Each room a wound, each shadow like a call.
The silence settled deeper than the pain.

I hated you, then missed you just the same,
Then hated how the ache could still enthrall.
You vanished, and the stillness made it plain.

Now quiet is the keeper of your name,
A voice that echoes from an empty hall.
The silence settled deeper than the pain.
You vanished, and the stillness made it plain.

February, Unsent
by Liliana Caliente-Cazadora

Feb 1
I changed my sheets.
Pretended that made a difference.

Feb 3
Deleted your number.
Still remember it. Muscle memory is cruel.

Feb 5
Laughed at a meme, then wanted to send it to you.
Forgot halfway through that I can't.
Did it hurt less last week, or am I just tired today?

Feb 7
Everyone says healing isn't linear.
Today I circled the drain.
Tomorrow I'll try for the edge again.

Feb 9
You posted a picture.
You look like you slept well.
I didn't.

Feb 11
Valentine's displays everywhere.
Bought myself roses.
Thorns still drew blood.

Feb 14
Didn't cry.
Didn't call.

Didn't win. Didn't lose.
Just existed.

Feb 17
Dreamt of you.
Woke up angry.
Stayed that way.

Feb 21
Talked to someone new.
Laughed without checking if it made sense.
That felt like something.

Feb 23
Silence isn't heavy anymore.
It's just there. Like the wind.

Feb 26
I didn't think of you today.
Then I did.
But only for a second.

Feb 28
I made it through the month.
Still miss you.
But I'm starting to miss me less.

Spiral
by Liliana Caliente-Cazadora

I miss you.
I miss the way you laughed when you weren't thinking.
I miss how we fit like a sentence and its silence.
I miss what we almost became.

I miss the sound of your voice in the morning.
I miss the way I never had to explain myself.
I miss the version of me who was enough for you.
I miss the stories we never got to write.

I miss you like a song with no end.
I miss you like I miss who I was with you.
I miss you like I shouldn't.

I miss you on Tuesdays.
I miss you in doorways.
I miss you in the pause between my inhale
and everything I don't say out loud.

I miss the quiet after your name.
I miss the text I don't send.
I miss the hope I keep folding
like a note I'll never pass.

I miss you.
I miss you again.
I miss the idea of you.
I miss me
when I missed you
less.

SECTION V:
What Remains and What Matters
**Speaks to the idea of sorting through
pain and finding what's worth keeping.**

This Is How I Begin Again
by Liliana Caliente-Cazadora

Not with fireworks,
or some bold proclamation.
Just a quiet morning
where I don't ache
the way I used to.

The tea is warm.
The silence is kind.
And my reflection
looks like someone
I'm learning to trust again.

I no longer check my phone
for your name.
Not because I've stopped missing you—
but because I've stopped waiting.

Some healing happens
loudly.
Mine came like
a letter I wrote
to myself—
gently folded,
tucked into the lining of my chest,
and carried
until it felt like truth.

This is how I begin again:
By breathing.
By showing up.
By remembering
that being whole

was never supposed to depend on
someone else staying.

Things I've Learned Without You
by Liliana Caliente-Cazadora

I've learned
that silence can be sacred
when it's not waiting
to be broken.

That love
should never feel
like holding my breath.

That I can miss you
and still move forward.
Both are true.
Both are allowed.

I've learned
to sleep on my side
without reaching for what isn't there,
to make my own coffee
just the way I like it.
You never got it right anyway.

I've learned
that healing doesn't mean
forgetting—
it means remembering
without bleeding.

That I am not
what you left behind.
I am
what I picked up afterward.

And I've learned, finally,
that I was never asking for too much.
I was just asking the wrong person.

What I Never Needed After All
by Liliana Caliente-Cazadora

I used to think
your love was the prize—
the proof
that I was worth something.

But now I see it:
I was bending
just to fit inside
a story
you weren't even writing.

I confused your absence
with mystery.
I called your inconsistency
"freedom."

I mistook
your inability to love me well
as my own failure
to deserve it.

But I've grown quiet enough
to hear the truth:
you were never home—
just a place I passed through
hoping it would feel like one.

I don't hate you.
I don't want you back.
And most surprising of all,
I don't need to understand
why you left.

That's the freedom
I didn't know I needed.
And now
I do.

To the Version of Me Who Stayed Too Long
by Liliana Caliente-Cazadora

I'm sorry
for all the nights
you begged for love
from someone
who only gave you
just enough
to keep you hoping.

I'm sorry
for the way you softened
when you should have stood tall,
for how you twisted yourself
into someone easier to leave.

I'm sorry
you thought it was your fault—
that their silence
meant you weren't worth hearing.

You weren't weak.
You were loyal.
You weren't broken.
You were brave.

You weren't too much.
They just weren't ready
for the kind of love
you carried.

I see you now—
tired eyes,
open heart,

still hoping for someone
who'd meet you halfway.

You waited.
You forgave.
You tried.

Now it's my turn
to do that for you.

So here I am—
not to shame you,
but to thank you
for surviving
what I finally walked away from.

Soft Doesn't Mean Weak
by Liliana Caliente-Cazadora

I used to think
I had to be sharp
to survive.

Guarded.
Untouchable.
Unbreakable.

But healing taught me
something different—
that strength
is not the armor,
but the choice
to take it off.

Soft
is the voice that stays kind
even after the storm.
Soft
is the heart that still hopes
without begging.
Soft
is showing up
when you could've disappeared.

I am not less
because I feel everything.
I am not fragile
because I still believe in love.

There's power in staying open
when you've been shattered.

There's beauty
in rebuilding with tenderness.

So no—
I'm not hard anymore.
I'm not cold.
I'm not bitter.

I'm soft.
And I'm still here.
And that
is strength.

The Silence Feels Different Now
by Liliana Caliente-Cazadora

It used to echo.
Loud.
Sharp.
Like everything I didn't say
was shouting back at me.

I filled it with noise—
old songs,
unfinished texts,
fantasies of closure.

I was scared of what I might hear
if it got too quiet.
Scared the silence would tell me
it was my fault.
That I wasn't enough.

But now—
now the silence feels like space.
Like breath.
Like a room I finally cleaned
and left the window open for.

It no longer hurts.
It holds.

And in that stillness,
I don't hear your voice anymore.
I hear mine.

The Last Word I'll Never Send
by Liliana Caliente-Cazadora

I thought this story would end
with a reply.
An apology.
A second chance.
A door swinging open.

But instead,
it ends with me—
still standing.
Still soft.
Still whole
in the places that once shattered.

I kept too much inside,
held conversations in my bones
like they might keep me warm.
But bones don't speak,
and silence isn't safety.

So here it is—
the last word I'll never send:

Thank you.

Not for the heartbreak,
but for what I found beneath it.
The version of me
who doesn't beg to be seen,
doesn't chase closed doors,
doesn't need your voice
to remember her own.

I release you
in full,
in peace,
in poetry.

And now,
I return to myself.

About The Author

Liliana Caliente-Cazadora is a Latina author whose work explores the quiet ache of longing, the beauty of vulnerability, and the spaces between what's said and what's left behind. Born and raised in East Los Angeles, Liliana grew up surrounded by stories— spoken, whispered, and imagined—that continue to shape her voice today.

Known initially for her bold and sensual storytelling, Liliana has shifted toward more reflective and emotionally layered work, including poetry, romantic fiction, and literary pieces that honor the complexities of love, loss, and healing. Her writing blends raw honesty with lyrical tenderness, drawing readers into the kind of truths we rarely say out loud.

Now based in Denver, Colorado, she finds inspiration in mountain sunrises, local cafés, and the deep, transformative power of human connection. When she's not writing, she's reading romance novels, collecting notebooks she may never use, and occasionally texting things she'll never send.